For Shirley

Library of Congress Control Number: 2018936497

Text and pictures copyright © 2018 by James Stewart
First published in the United States of America
in 2018 by Albert Whitman & Company
ISBN 978-0-8075-7855-1

Printed in China
10 9 8 7 6 5 4 3 2 1 WKT 22 21 20 19 18

Design by James Stewart and Morgan Beck

For more information about Albert Whitman & Company,
visit our website at www.albertwhitman.com.

There's a Hole in my Garden

James Stewart

Albert Whitman & Company
Chicago, Illinois

January

I found a hole in my garden this morning.

It's not a very big hole.

But it's just the right size for my best marble,

so I dropped it into the hole.

I hope it will grow into a marble tree.

February

Marble trees don't grow overnight.

This one doesn't look like it's growing at all.

But the hole is—it's a little bigger now.

Maybe some candy will grow.

So I bought some and dropped it into the hole.

I hope it will grow into a candy tree.

March

The candy tree isn't growing either.

But the hole is now big enough for my flashlight.

When I dropped it into the hole, it fell down and down

until I couldn't see the light anymore.

I hope a flashlight tree will grow and fill up the hole.

April

No luck with the flashlight tree.

But the hole is now big enough that my robot

went straight in. I'm sorry I don't have it anymore,

but if I get a robot tree, it will be great.

May

No robot tree.

Just a really big hole.

I put in the piano.

Do piano trees grow?

I'm going to find out.

June

It looks like piano trees don't grow.

All I've got now is a bigger hole.

The dinosaur went straight in, no problem.

Soon I'll have a dinosaur tree.

July

There's no dinosaur tree.

But there is a really big hole.

That train drove right in.

August

You guessed it.

No train tree.

The hole is really big.

Big enough for a ship.

There might be a ship tree soon.

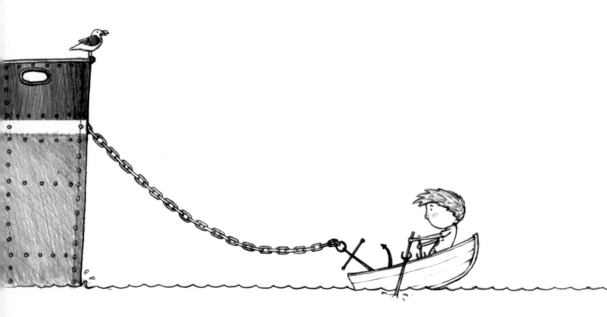

September

No ship tree.

The hole is so big that I could put a house in it.

So that's what I did.

October

No house tree, but the hole is HUGE.

It took the rocket, no problem.

A rocket tree would fill up that hole.

November

The hole has swallowed the garden.

I never knew a hole could be that big.

It wasn't easy, but in one month

there may be a moon tree

where the garden used to be.

December

No marble tree, no candy tree, no flashlight tree,

no robot tree, no piano tree, no dinosaur tree,

no train tree, no ship tree, no house tree,

no rocket tree, no moon tree.

Just the biggest hole in the world.

I looked in a book to figure out what to do.

The only thing that fits in a black hole is a star.

So that's what I did.

I caught the biggest star I could

and dropped it down that hole.

I can't wait to see my star tree.